SPOOK SCHOOL

LAIR OF THE MOTHMAN

PETE JOHNSON

Illustrated by
Tom Percival

Chapter One
The Floating Hand

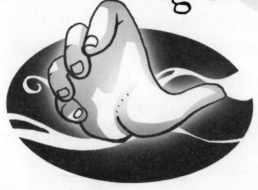

I rubbed my eyes and stared. Something
was floating towards me.

It was a hand.

"Whoah," I gasped.

I'd just woken up. I hadn't a clue
where I was. It was too dark to see much.
And now I'd been joined by a hand.

The hand started flying around me.

"Hi there, hand," I squeaked, ducking
out of the way.

To my great surprise the hand answered. "Oops, sorry. Now whatever you do, don't be frightened," it said.

"Of course not," I said to myself. "I'm in a weird place, with a talking hand for company – no reason to be frightened whatsoever."

The voice went on. "Get ready for the rest of me." The next moment a second hand appeared, then some legs and a body.

"How's that?" said the voice. It sounded quite proud of itself.

"Very good," I gasped. "It's just you're missing a head."

"Oh, I'm always forgetting that." The voice laughed and I sort of laughed too.

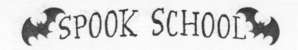

Seconds later a face oozed up out of the darkness. A friendly face belonging to a boy who looked about my age. He had smiley brown eyes and a big grin.

"I thought it would be less scary if you saw me in stages," he explained. "Er, seeing a floating hand was

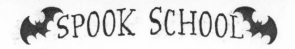

pretty scary actually," I said. And then I burped loudly. I always do that when I'm nervous.

"Sorry about that."

"No worries," he said cheerfully. "I'm Lewis."

"And are you…" I whispered the last word, "a ghost?"

He grinned. "That's what some people call us. But we prefer to be called spooks. It sounds much cooler, doesn't it?"

"I suppose it does," I said, grinning too. "Wow, I can't believe I'm really dreaming this – you seem so real. It's the best dream I've had for years. So tell me, Lewis, what it's like being a ghost, sorry, spook?"

"It's just brilliant," he began. "You get to float through doors and make things appear out of nowhere." But then he started shaking his head. "No, I'm doing this all wrong. This is my first time as a welcome spook and I totally forgot to tell you…"

"Tell me what?"

He looked right at me. "That you're a spook, too."

I tried to laugh. "Me a spook, too!
Of course I'm not."

"It's true, Charlie," he said quietly.

"How do you know my name?"
I asked, surprised.

"I was sent by the Spookmaster to
collect you. He told me all about you."

I gaped at him. "I'm sorry, I still
think you're making all this up. Can
you prove I'm a spook?"

12

"Oh yes," said Lewis. "Just touch your arm."

I reached out – and got the shock of my life. It was as if I'd seized hold of a piece of ice.

"But I'm freezing cold," I cried.

"All spooks are permanently freezing," said Lewis, "and when we get frightened we become even colder."

I stared into the darkness. "Where am I?" I asked.

"On top of a hill – where new spooks always arrive to be collected."

He crouched down beside me. "You'll love being a spook. We have brilliant lessons."

"Lessons," I spluttered. "Don't tell me spooks have to go to school."

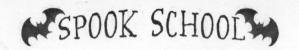

"Oh yes," said Lewis.

"Well, I'm not." I folded my arms. "I hate school and I'm not doing any more lessons, ever."

Lewis grinned. "At Spook School we don't do boring lessons like Maths. We do stuff like learning how to fly."

"Really," I muttered, trying not to sound impressed.

"And guess what?" went on Lewis.

"What?" I said.

"A few of the top spooks are chosen to go off on secret missions," he explained. "They're called the Spook Squad. Two of these spooks are on a mission right now, investigating the strange case of…" he lowered his voice to a whisper, "Mothman."

I leaned forward. "So what's that?"

"A very scary creature who's haunting a house. It's a moth…"

"Oh, big deal," I said. "Fancy being scared of a moth."

"A moth the size of a horse," said Lewis.

"What?" I gasped.

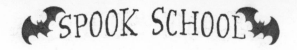

Lewis grinned triumphantly. "It's also got really sharp claws and a very bad temper. It has taken over a house and it terrifies any human who tries to come inside. We've nicknamed it Mothman."

"Cool," I said. "I'd love to go off chasing monsters."

Lewis nodded eagerly. "Me too."

Suddenly a horrible, terrifying wail filled the air.

"What's that?" I asked, my voice shaking.

"That's just the school howl," said Lewis. "It means lessons are about to start." Then he threw back his head and let out an answering howl.

Ooooh!

"They like it if you howl back," he said, "then they know you're on your way."

"But it's nearly dark," I said. "Funny time for lessons to start."

"Oh, we find we're at our brightest at night," said Lewis. "Are you coming?"

I hesitated. "Where is this school? Is it far?"

"It is if you're walking, but not if you're floating."

"And how do I float?"

"That can be tricky for new spooks. But don't worry, I've got an idea."

Lewis let out a low whistle.

A couple of seconds later he was smiling and saying, "Good boy, I knew you wouldn't let me down."

The trouble was – no one was there. Lewis was talking to the air.

"Lewis," I said, "what exactly are you doing?"

"After you've been at Spook School

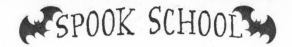

for a while you're allowed a pet. I'm talking to Star, my horse, the best horse in the whole world; a stallion, who flies like the wind."

I stared at him. "But there's nothing there."

"Yes there is – he's invisible though."

"An invisible horse? Oh, of course, I really do believe you."

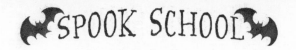

"But he's here. You can pat him. Look, see for yourself."

I edged forward and then gave a tremble of surprise. He was right, I could touch Star. And he felt exactly like a normal horse – only quite a bit chillier.

"Now climb up," said Lewis. "He's very gentle, so you'll be fine."

I don't know if you've ever tried climbing on to an invisible horse, but it's a bit tricky. Star kept giving impatient little neighs as if to say, "Hurry up."

"Whisper to him when you're ready to go," said Lewis, adding, "he knows the way to Spook School."

So I whispered, "Star, let's go to Spook School." And immediately he took off, with Lewis floating beside us.

"I bet you've never gone to school on an invisible horse before," said Lewis.

"I can honestly say I haven't," I cried, as Star sped along even faster.

"Well, this is just the start," cried Lewis. "You've got lots more surprises ahead."

Chapter Three

Learning to Float

When we reached the school Star gave a loud neigh. Then I felt his face nuzzling lightly against mine.

"He only usually does that to me," said Lewis. "He must like you."

I jumped down and looked around. First, all I could see was a thick blanket of icy, cold fog. It hung over everything. Then, just for a moment, a white moon glided through the haze, and I saw a huge grey building, sparkling and glittering in the silver moonlight. It looked absolutely bursting with magic. But then the moon disappeared and everything was covered in mist again.

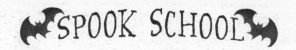

"Follow me," said Lewis, his voice muffled by the fog.

"I can hardly see where I'm going," I cried.

"I know," said Lewis. "The fog makes everything so exciting, doesn't it? But you wouldn't want to get lost around here."

I was about to ask why not, when I heard a door creak open and seconds later I followed Lewis into a dark corridor. I could see spooks – some younger than me – floating up and down the corridor. The windows were dark and dusty and there were cobwebs everywhere. "They let us decorate the school," said Lewis. "And we wanted to make it look as cheerful as possible."

Cobwebs – cheerful! The windows were slightly open so the fog oozed into the school, too. I shivered. This felt more like a house in a horror film.

"So it really is a school?" I asked nervously.

Lewis laughed. "Oh yeah, only we call the teachers ghouls, except the headmaster, he's Spookmaster. He can be a bit scary so try not to annoy him."

"I'll try," I said. "But sometimes teachers annoy me."

Lewis looked at me doubtfully and whispered, "Whatever you do, don't upset the Spookmaster. For when he gets angry – well, it's definitely not a pretty sight. I'll take you to your classroom."

He led me down this dark, eerie corridor, covered with cobwebs.

☙SPOOK SCHOOL☙

At the end, a wooden door creaked
open and a woman with jet black hair
and the largest eyes I've ever seen
leaped out in front of us.
"Ah, you must be the
new spook,
Charlie."

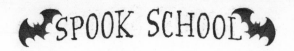

"That's me," I said.

"Welcome to Spook School. I'm Ghoul One," she announced. "And here's your timetable." She handed me a piece of paper which looked like an ancient parchment. And on it, in very faint writing, were things like: "Floating for Beginners", and "How to Fly".

"See you later," whispered Lewis. Then he added, "Oh, in your floating lesson – believe you can do it and you will. It's that simple."

"Yeah, right," I said, as I followed Ghoul One inside.

I was in a very odd classroom. There were no desks and chairs, just tons of cushions on the floor which the other spooks were sitting on.

"We believe spooks learn best when they're relaxed," said Ghoul One. "Now spooks, say hello to Charlie in our friendly way."

All the spooks put back their heads and made a very similar noise to the school howl.

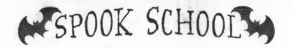

"Why don't you try that, Charlie?" she said.

So I took a deep breath and let out a really blood-curdling howl.

Ghoul One clapped her hands in delight. "Oh yes, I'm sure you'll soon settle in."

I slouched on one of the cushions – it was very soft and comfortable. I grinned at the other spooks; some of them looked younger than me.

Then came our first lesson: floating. Ghoul One said, "I want you to see if you can rise up one metre today. This won't be easy." She babbled on giving instructions, but I quickly stopped listening. Why do all teachers talk so much? Instead I remembered what

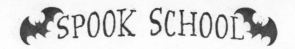

Lewis had said to me. So I closed my eyes tight, I pictured myself floating and then said, "Spook-float."

At once I had the feeling of great energy building up inside me. But when I opened my eyes, I was still sitting on the floor. I closed my eyes once more and imagined myself floating again. And this time I concentrated really hard as I said, "Spook-float." Then, with a little *whoosh* I was off, and when I opened my eyes I saw that I was a metre off the ground.

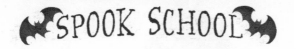

"Wow, this is good fun," I cried.

"Oh, well done, Charlie," called
Ghoul One, "you're skimming along
nicely already. That's terrific. Everyone
watch Charlie."

I was feeling stronger and more
confident with every second. And
that's when it happened. All at once I
soared right up to the ceiling. How
cool was that? The other spooks gaped
at me. Some of them were still
flapping their arms trying to get off
the ground.

Then I started wiggling my bottom
about. The spooks began to laugh. So I
wiggled it some more. Next I began
diving up and down in the air. The
spooks clapped and laughed.

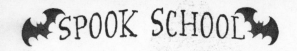

"That's enough now, Charlie, we don't like show-offs," warned Ghoul One. "Come back down, please."

But instead of doing what I was told, I flew quickly round the whole classroom, still wiggling my bottom as I went. Then I noticed one of the windows was open. I only meant to take a little peek outside, but it was hard to see anything with all that fog pouring everywhere. Before I could stop myself, I'd flown right out of the window.

The next thing I knew I was sailing straight up into the dark night sky. All at once I could see through the fog and make out the stars glittering and shining ahead of me. It was amazing – until I looked down.

"Whoah!" I cried, clutching at the air, and feeling very, very sick. Suddenly I started to tumble down … down … down, burping all the way. With a sharp *whoosh* I landed just outside my classroom.

I looked up to see all my class and Ghoul One standing outside and gazing anxiously at me.

"No new spook has ever flown so high before," Ghoul One began excitedly. "And I told you not to do that," she added sternly.

Before I could reply another spook floated over to her. He whispered something I couldn't catch.

Ghoul One looked very serious. "Charlie, the Spookmaster wants to see you immediately."

Chapter Four
The Spookmaster

Ghoul One skimmed down the corridor. I had to run to keep up. There was just one tiny candle lighting the way, and the fog was so thick, it seemed to wrap itself around me. The cobwebs were everywhere, too. I kept flying into them. "Am I in trouble?" I asked.

Ghoul One looked at me. "You must stop showing off, Charlie. Spookmaster hates show-offs."

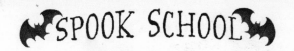
SPOOK SCHOOL

We stopped outside the very last door in the corridor.

"Give a loud howl and wait to hear an answering one from inside," said Ghoul One.

I threw back my head and howled. And from inside came a really fierce sound – more like a hungry wolf than a spook. "He sounds happy," I said, trying to smile.

Ghoul One smiled back. "Goodbye, Charlie," she whispered. "Take care."

I stared at her. What did she mean "Goodbye"? But before I could ask she'd vanished into thin air. How awesome to be able to disappear so fast. I hoped I'd learn how to do that soon.

Meanwhile the Spookmaster's door

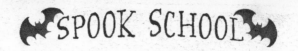

seemed to be opening by itself. It creaked and moaned as if trying to say, "Run for your life."

I stepped inside. "H-h-hello," I whispered to the empty room.

Suddenly a voice boomed, "Goodnight, Charlie." I looked up and there was the Spookmaster, sitting cross-legged right above my head. "I find I can think better up here," he explained. He was extremely old, with red, fluffy hair and two very stern eyes. He wore a large, flapping gown just like the ones teachers wore in olden times. He looked like an extremely fierce, incredibly ancient lion.

"Join me," he commanded in a loud, sharp voice.

So I closed my eyes and said, "Spook-float," and sailed up into the air beside him.

He glared at me. "Stop looking so pleased with yourself. You disobeyed Ghoul One, didn't you?"

I hung my head.

"Now here's a real test for you." He pointed towards the door. "I want you to fly right through that."

I burped. "Oops! Sorry about that," I said at once. Then I added, "You want me to fly right through—"

"Yes, yes," he interrupted. "Just get on with it. Concentrate hard and say 'Spook-fly' three times."

"I'll give it a try," I said, "but I—"

"Stop talking and do it," he ordered.

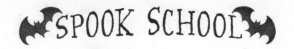

"OK, OK," I muttered. I hated it when teachers shouted at me. And they were always doing that at my old school. I floated towards the door, then I closed my eyes and said, "Spook-fly," three times. I flew towards the door until I was hovering just in front of it. "You can do this," I said to myself. I imagined myself gliding through the door, and I could feel the power inside me growing stronger and stronger.

Then it was like that moment when you first dive into freezing cold water. My whole body twitched with horror. But I'd done it.

I stood outside the Spookmaster's door, gasping and shivering – yet I couldn't help grinning, too. I was so

43

proud of myself. I'd flown through a door. Skilful or what?!

"Now come back in again," barked the Spookmaster from the other side.

It wasn't quite so hard the second time, but it still made me shudder a bit.

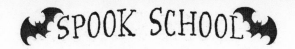

I was feeling really pleased with myself, until I saw the Spookmaster's stern face. He loomed in front of me. Didn't he ever smile? He was also very tall indeed. "Only one other spook managed to do that on their first day," he said. "Do you know who that was?"

"Lewis," I suggested.

"No," he replied. "Me."

"So I'm as good as you already," I cried eagerly.

"I did not say that. You seem to have remarkable powers, but you have much to learn. This is not a game, Charlie. And you must use your gifts wisely. Do you understand?"

"Yes, Mr Spookmaster."

"You only need address me as

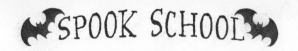

Spookmaster," he said. Then he went on, "In the past you have got into trouble at school, like that time you shouted out 'Smelly knickers' in assembly."

"That was a dare," I began. Then I stopped. "How do you know about that?"

"I know all about you," he said solemnly. "We cannot have that kind of behaviour here. Is that clear?"

I nodded.

"Good. You will not be returning to your class again."

So that was why Ghoul One had said "goodbye" to me. But where was I going?

"Instead," went on the Spookmaster, "you will be joining the top class."

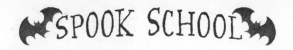

"Oh wow," I cried, "that's amazing!"

"It is," said the Spookmaster. "In fact, only one other spook pupil has ever gone from the junior class to the top class in one night."

"You," I suggested.

"Me," he agreed.

Just then two spooks charged through the Spookmaster's door. They looked very upset. "We let you down, Spookmaster," burst out the first one.

"Mothman was just too terrifying," said the other. "He is the scariest creature we've ever seen."

The first spook nodded. "It snarled and snapped and then it just charged towards us ... a creature out of your worst nightmare."

47

"Only smellier," said the other. "It
absolutely stank."

I giggled. I couldn't help it. It
sounded so funny. A stinky monster.
For the first time they spotted me.

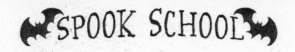

"Oh, sorry, Spookmaster," they chorused. "We didn't know you were interviewing a new spook."

"That's all right," said Spookmaster, with a surprisingly kindly look on his wrinkled face. "You tried your best – and that's all anyone can ask." Then he turned to me. "These are two of my best spooks. I sent them down to investigate a creature known as Mothman. But it has terrified even them, the bravest members of Spook Squad." He sighed. "I will have to think what to do next."

"Maybe I could help," I said eagerly. "Lewis has already told me all about Mothman, and a giant moth with a bad attitude wouldn't bother me in the least."

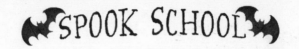

I thought Spookmaster might scold me for showing off. But instead a tiny flicker of a smile crossed his ancient face, and he said softly but firmly, "Off you float, Charlie."

"OK," I said. "But if you change your mind about Mothman, just howl as I'd love to meet him."

Chapter Five

In Trouble Again

In case you're wondering, spooks do sleep.

But they sleep standing up. And of course they go to sleep in the daytime.

That morning my head was still buzzing from all the excitement of my first night at Spook School. I stood in the dormitory in the middle of a row of spooks, with Lewis on one side of me, but I wasn't in the least bit sleepy.

I'll never be able to sleep like this, I thought, as the spook on my other side began to snore gently.

I whispered to Lewis, "I'm not at all tired, are you?" Then I noticed how much paler he seemed. All of a sudden I could see right through him. And then he started to vanish completely.

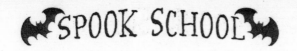

"Lewis," I called, alarmed.

"It's all right, I'm still here," murmured Lewis. "Spooks become very hard to see when they're asleep."

"Sleep well then," I said, a bit annoyed, "because I know I won't."

"Oh yes you will," whispered Lewis. "Try counting cobwebs…"

A few minutes later I felt myself drifting away, too. When I woke up it was late in the afternoon and Lewis, now completely visible again, was grinning at me. "I thought you weren't sleepy," he said. "Come on, Charlie, it's getting dark, so time for us to get busy." Then he looked at me and added, "By the way, you can change into different clothes if you want."

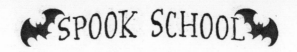

"Can I?" I looked down. I was wearing my old school uniform for some reason.

"Of course, just think about what you'd like to wear and say, "Spook-clothes.""

"Well, I'm not really bothered what I look like. But I really like that jacket you're wearing – it's dead cool."

Lewis looked very pleased. "Well, go ahead and copy it if you want."

So I did.

We went off and played floating football, which was brilliant fun. I got chatting with some of the other spooks, including Jasmine, who is a real laugh and Paul, who is apparently Ghoul One's pet.

And now I never walked at all,

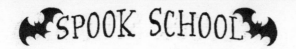

I floated everywhere. Gliding along in the air is so relaxing. It was definitely one of the best things about being a spook.

Then the howl sounded for the start of lessons. Before, I hated school. Well, I was bottom of the class at just about everything. But now I was in the top group with Lewis. And today we were practising how to appear and disappear – cool or what?

The other spooks had already started work on this. But I soon caught them up – all except Lewis. He could disappear in the blink of an eye. It was incredible.

Returning was much harder, though. You had to say "Spook-return" while concentrating really hard. First of all,

it's just your right hand which appears.
So anyone peeping into our classroom
at that moment would have seen
thirty hands dancing about
all by themselves.

Then it's your left hand, followed by
your body. Once again, Lewis was the
fastest. Even if he did keep forgetting
his head – just as he did the very first
day I met him.

Jasmine yelled at him, "Lewis, you're
headless again."

☾SPOOK SCHOOL☽

Then we had a lesson on how to make small objects move. This takes great concentration. You have to shut out all other thoughts and say to yourself, "Spook-move." It's great though when you do get, say, a vase to skim over to you.

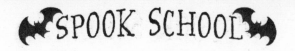

SPOOK SCHOOL

Our teacher, who was called Top Ghoul, was young and very energetic. She said tomorrow we were going to have a lesson on how to make things appear out of nowhere – starting with a leaf. But now she was going to tell us a story about spooks who used their power for good. Only I didn't want to listen to that. I wanted to make things appear out of nowhere NOW.

And it wouldn't be a leaf either, as that was far too boring. What about a spider instead? Yeah, brilliant.

So while everyone else sat around on cushions listening to the story I closed my eyes. "Spook-spider show yourself." I imagined this so clearly I thought I was going to burst.

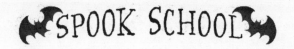

And then I opened my eyes and saw a little spider scuttling about on the ground. I was so proud, as I'd made it all by myself. I nudged Lewis. "Look," I pointed. "All my own work."

"Wow," he whispered. "Cool."

"Shall I make the spider a bit bigger?" I whispered.

"No, better not," said Lewis. Then he grinned. "Oh, go on then."

So I closed my eyes and focused on the spider. "Spook-spider, be the biggest spider anyone has ever seen."

We gazed down and saw this absolutely huge, hairy spider sitting on the floor in front of us. Jasmine saw it too, and nearly let out a cry of horror.

"It's all right," I said. "It's with me."

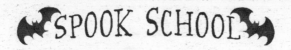

Then I saw Lewis tremble beside me. "That spider looks so mean, I bet it stings, too. Vanish it away fast."

And I was about to when I noticed Ghoul One's pet, Paul. He certainly never did anything wrong. And now he was listening to the story as if it was the best tale he'd ever heard. In fact, he had his mouth wide open. I decided I'd give him a little surprise.

So I closed my eyes again. "Spook-spider, start climbing up Paul's leg."

"What are you doing?" gasped Lewis.

"Watch," I grinned.

Moments later my massive spider began scuttling up Paul's leg. Lewis gasped and shrieked

61

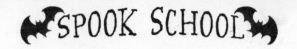

all at the same time.

Paul glanced down. For a moment he couldn't believe his eyes.

Then he let out the loudest scream you've ever heard.

And I was in so much trouble.

Chapter Six
Blood!

I was grounded for a whole hour. So while everyone else was off playing floating football, I had to sit in this dim little room, thinking about what I'd done wrong. And even worse, my feet weren't allowed to leave the ground. Funny how quickly you get used to soaring off everywhere.

As soon as the hour was up, Spookmaster appeared in the doorway, huge and terrifying. He was so angry with me that tiny globules of steam were coming out of his hair. "Do not waste your talent on being silly," he boomed. "Is that clear?"

"Totally clear, Spookmaster," I replied. He didn't say anything else, but his eyes went on boring into me and clouds of steam emerged from his face. This went on for ages, but even I didn't dare speak. At last he said, "Never let it happen again, Charlie."

I nodded my head solemnly.

Then I whispered, "Spookmaster, I just wondered, have you found anyone to tackle Mothman yet?"

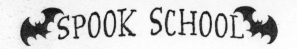

He gave me a curious look. "Yes, Charlie, I have. Two people in fact."

At once I felt really jealous. And as soon as Spookmaster dismissed me I hurried to tell Lewis.

"I'd love to have the chance to meet Mothman," I sighed.

Lewis grinned. "Well, you'll have to stop getting into trouble first."

The following day in class we had to practise making leaves appear. All the other spooks – even Lewis – found this difficult. But I found it really easy.

So later in the dormitory I gave the spooks an extra lesson. Then Lewis tried again. "I've done it," he cried as he finally conjured up a leaf – and

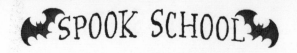

watched it drift slowly to the ground.

Then a spook called Richie, who can be nearly as mischievous as me said, "Go on then, make another spider appear, Charlie."

"No, don't, please don't," squeaked Paul. "You know I hate spiders."

"OK," I said, "no more spiders. Has anyone got any other suggestions?"

And they had. Tons of them – an apple, a mouth organ … then Richie said, "How about a drop of blood?"

"All right," I cried. "If it's blood you want, just watch. You will now see a drop of blood dripping down our door."

My head was buzzing. I could hardly hold in my excitement, but I knew I had to concentrate. So I closed my eyes and said, "Spook-blood, loads of blood." I don't know why I said that last bit. Well I do, I was showing off. Again. I opened my eyes just as a large drop of bright red blood slithered its way down the door and landed with a plop on the floor.

Everyone clapped – and I bowed, enjoying all the attention. Then we waited for the blood to vanish. Only it didn't, instead it lay on the floor, glistening and shining. Then, to my horror, another even larger drop of blood started streaking down the door. And then another, and another.

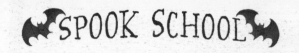

Soon the drops had joined together to make a small pond.

"Make it stop," said Paul, beginning to panic.

I quickly closed my eyes and said, "Spook-blood, go." But I was so worried I couldn't concentrate properly.

And when I opened my eyes the blood was still there. Only now it was running down the door ... and the small pond on the floor was in danger of turning into a river.

"Charlie! Do something," cried Lewis.

"Don't worry," I said, trying to give everyone a winning smile. "I'm sure I can make it stop this time."

But I couldn't.

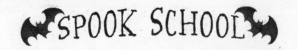

"I think we ought to get someone," said Paul.

At that very moment something flew through the door at an incredible speed.

It was the Spookmaster.

Oh no. Now I was in trouble.

But instead of sending me to detention, he just hovered there looking at me. "You have the power in you to stop this. Just believe that." His voice was surprisingly quiet, but still very commanding. I closed my eyes and tried again, concentrating really hard. Within seconds there was a small cheer.

I opened my eyes; the blood had completely vanished.

Then the Spookmaster said, "I shall

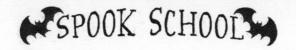

see you and Lewis in my room immediately."

"Oh, not Lewis," I said quickly. "He had nothing to do with it. This is all my fault."

"I will see you both in my room," repeated the Spookmaster. And he floated through the door with Lewis and me rushing anxiously after him.

"Sorry," I whispered to Lewis, thinking we were about to get a massive telling-off.

"Don't worry," he said. "Seeing all that blood was brilliant."

The Spookmaster flew off at such a speed, we had to work really hard to keep up with him. Inside his room he immediately glided up into the air.

"Charlie, you behaved foolishly again tonight. But I hope you have finally learned your lesson."

"Oh, I have," I said at once.

"I am glad to hear it," said the Spookmaster, "because I have an important announcement to make."

Chapter Seven

Off on a Mission

"Both of you," went on Spookmaster, "have great powers."

"Oh, we know that…" I began.

But then Lewis hissed, "Be quiet! Spookmaster hates show-offs." I didn't say another word after that.

"But you still have much to learn," Spookmaster continued, "such as shape changing."

"What's that?" asked Lewis.

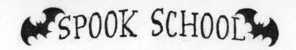

"A few especially talented spooks have the ability to change shape," he explained. "This takes great skill – and a lot of practice. But don't worry about that now, you already have many powers and I think you are both ready to join Spook Squad and take part in your first ever mission."

Lewis and I grinned at each other in delight. Then I punched the air. "Yes!"

Spookmaster glared down at me. "You must control yourself, Charlie," he thundered.

"Sorry, Mr Spookmaster. I mean, Spookmaster," I gabbled. "I'm just so excited. What are we going to do?"

"I want you," said Spookmaster, "to investigate a USC."

"Don't you mean a UFO?" I asked. "Excuse me for correcting you," I added hastily.

"No," said Spookmaster. "I mean an Unidentified Spooky Creature, which has been observed in an old house in Hertfordshire."

"You don't mean Mothman?" I cried. Spookmaster nodded slowly.

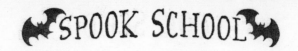

"But that's brilliant," I said, just stopping myself from punching the air again. Lewis, too, was floating about excitedly.

"Listen to me very carefully," said Spookmaster. "There are some spooks who want to go on residing on Earth. So we allow them to haunt houses, although we do try and discourage them from clanking chains and groaning. Yet, we have no record of a spook haunting Number 1 Rye Road in Hertfordshire."

"But something is there?" said Lewis.

"Definitely," said Spookmaster. "And we need to know what it is. Is it a spook or a human? Whatever it is, it has terrified several humans – and two of my top spooks."

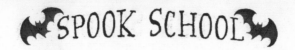

"It won't scare us," I said.

Spookmaster smiled faintly. "We shall see," he murmured. "We need to get to the bottom of it. So it is your mission to find out what this creature is up to – and report back. Are you willing to take up the challenge?"

"Of course we are," I said.

"And what do you have to say, Lewis?"

"I'll go, of course I will," said Lewis eagerly.

"Good," he said, "because you are the leader of this mission."

"Oh." Almost without thinking I let out a cry of surprise.

"So, Charlie, you will have to take orders from Lewis at all times," he said. "Do you think you can manage that?"

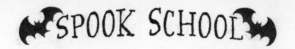

"Yes," I said at once.

"Are you sure?" he persisted.

"Of course, we're the best of friends," I said. "When do we leave?"

"Tomorrow night," said Spookmaster, as he flew even further up into the air. "And the very best of luck on this highly important mission."

Outside we flew round and round, mad with excitement.

"Can you believe it?" I cried. "We're off on a special mission for Spook Squad."

"And I'm the leader," shouted Lewis.

"That's right," I said, a little less excitedly.

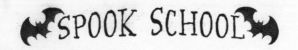

The next twenty-four hours just crawled past.

But finally it was time to go, and all our classmates stood in a row to see us off. The spooks wished us luck in the usual way; they gave one enormous howl. It sounded like a hundred hungry wolves. And although it was meant to be friendly, it was quite scary, too.

All at once I was nervous, so to keep my spirits (!) up, I yelled, "Now it's your turn to be scared, Mothman."

Top Ghoul floated down beside us. "As soon as you're ready, say 'Spook-travel' and think hard of where you're going. If for a moment your mind wanders," she warned, "and you start thinking about, say, the Eiffel Tower,

you might find you have landed there
instead; so complete concentration is
essential."

Lewis and I looked at each other.
"Ready?" asked Lewis.

"Absolutely," I replied.

I closed my eyes and said, "Spook-
travel to 1 Rye Road,

Hertfordshire." Then I kept

repeating the address over

and over.

Suddenly it was as if I'd slipped down this giant slide: I tumbled further and further at such a speed I burped loudly. It was like being on a never-ending fairground ride. All the time, I kept chanting, "1 Rye Road, Hertfordshire."

"Are we nearly there yet?" I called across to Lewis.

"Don't talk, concentrate," said Lewis.

On and on we hurtled and I tell you, it's lucky ghosts don't eat, because I'd have thrown up all over myself – just as I'd seen someone do on the waltzers once.

Then, after I'd chanted "1 Rye Road, Hertfordshire," for the nine hundredth time, I fell forward with a massive jolt and realized we'd arrived. I was back on Earth. And there was Lewis, floating beside me.

It was a grey, still night and somewhere a clock chimed midnight. Lewis pointed to a sign on our left that said Rye Road. We had landed outside the first house on the left – No. 1.

"When spooks travel," I said, "they definitely get door to door service."

"Only the best for us," grinned Lewis. Then he grew serious. "So here's our plan. We rush in there. Don't give ourselves time to get scared. Not that we will be anyway."

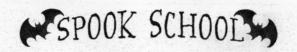

"Oh no," I agreed.

"Then we find out as quickly as we can what's going on in the haunted house. And we tell the monster or whatever it is to start behaving itself."

"It's a great plan," I said. "Let's go."

"Come on then," said Lewis flying ahead of me.

We raced up to the house. Paint was peeling from the window frames and there were weeds right up to the door. It looked gloomy and neglected.

We sailed through the front door and peered around. Cobwebs hung thickly in the air.

"Look at all those brilliant cobwebs," began Lewis. "Makes you feel right at home, doesn't it?"

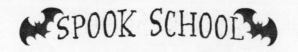

"They're awesome," I agreed. Then I started in surprise. Just a few nights ago I'd have hated cobwebs. But now I thought they really cheered up a house. I guessed that meant I was turning into a real spook.

"I'm feeling really good about this investigation," I began. Then I stopped. "Eeew, what's that terrible pong?"

Then Lewis smelt it, too. He clutched at his throat. It was like the smelliest, stalest, cheesiest socks in the world, magnified one million times.

I'd never smelt anything more disgusting.

"Spookmaster said no humans have dared come in here for ages," said Lewis. "Every time someone tries they're scared off by Mothman – and the stink, probably. Still, it won't bother us at all, will it?"

"Of course it won't," I said. But really I was feeling more and more uneasy. I sensed something bad was waiting for us. I gave a loud spook howl, just to stop myself getting any more nervous.

And right away came an answering cry: a great roar.

It was the kind of roar an elephant might make just before it charges at you; only much louder. And much, much angrier.

Long after it had finished, the noise still shuddered and shivered in my head. I peered around for Lewis, but he'd gone.　　　　　I sped after him.

He was hovering outside the house, shivering.

"You're as white as a ghost."

He tried to smile at that. "I can't

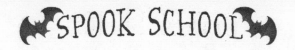

believe I was so spooked. But the noise it made…"

"I've never heard anything like it. It was even worse than the pong. We have to go back though," I said.

Lewis nodded.

But neither of us moved.

"Come on," said Lewis at once, "we're the Spook Squad. We mustn't let a few sound effects scare us."

"After you then," I said. "You are the leader after all."

"All right," said Lewis. "Only make sure you're right behind me at all times."

"Don't worry, I will be," I said. Then I added, trying to sound braver than I felt, "So let's go and say hi to the smelly Mothman."

Chapter Eight

A Horrifying Encounter

The roaring noise had come from the back of the house; I guessed that was where the kitchen was. So that was where we went first. "Here goes," said Lewis, diving through the door. I flew after him.

It was a huge kitchen but with hardly anything in it, just a table and chair – and no monster.

Or was there?

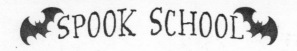

The room was full of deep shadows. Was the monster crouched in the darkness? Was he waiting for the right moment to strike?

"I don't think Mothman's here," whispered Lewis. "Maybe we frightened it away," he added hopefully.

"Well, we are quite scary spooks for our age," I said.

But we both stared uneasily into the darkness. And then one of the shadows stirred, right in the corner of the room.

"Did you see that?" I hissed.

"What?" asked Lewis.

"I think I saw something move."

"I didn't see anything," said Lewis. "Perhaps you just imagined it."

"Maybe," I agreed.

Then out of nowhere
came a really blood-
curdling screech.

I turned even colder.
"I didn't imagine that," I said.

"No, you didn't," Lewis gulped.

Then, just for a second I saw two
eyes spring out of the darkness. They
were bright yellow and seemed to burn
right through me. I was too petrified
to move.

Suddenly Mothman gave another
dreadful cry and dived right at me. The
creature had massive great wings, and it
was enormous. A giant moth all right.
Then I glimpsed its horrible, pinched
face. And razor sharp, glittering teeth. A
drop of blood trickled off its tongue.

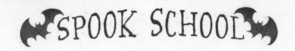

It gave another terrible cry, and stale, stinky air poured out of its mouth. Then it started chasing me round the room, its wings making a sharp breeze as it got nearer and nearer.

"It's going to gobble me up," I yelled. "Help!"

Then I heard Lewis shriek. "And now it's after me," he cried. Mothman gave a great roar of triumph, its teeth snapping and snarling as it turned on Lewis.

"Do something!" he yelled.

"Like what?" I cried.

Lewis didn't answer for a second, and then as Mothman charged at him again he screeched, "Let's get out of here!" I didn't argue.

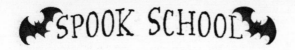

So once again we fled through the front door. But this time we didn't stop. This time we flew right up the road and didn't slow down until we'd reached the old railway station.

Now, when spooks rush past you, you won't see a thing, but you might just notice a sudden rush of air. And that night, as we streaked past an elderly couple on the platform, the man said, "Getting a bit breezy, isn't it?"

We sat shivering and shuddering a little further down the platform.

"I can't believe how huge it was," cried Lewis, his teeth chattering. "Or how stinky."

"Or how terrifying," I added. "And it almost got us, too."

But then Lewis said, "At least it couldn't have done anything to us."

"What!" I cried. "Are you mad! Why, it could have…" and then I stopped.

Lewis looked at me and smiled. "We're spooks, so what can it do?"

"You're right," I said.

"And anyway," Lewis cried, "we

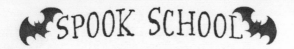

could have just vanished. We didn't
have to dash out of there like a couple
of frightened rabbits."

"But when I saw it I got so
terrified," I said, "that I forgot all that."

"So did I," said Lewis.

"I suppose that's what happened
to the other Spook Squad members,
too," I said.

We were silent for a moment. "Fancy
being scared by an overgrown moth," I
said at last, "for that's all it is. Well,
tonight we'll go back there and show
Mothman that spooks can make your
blood run cold, too. Actually, it probably
hasn't got any blood, but you know
what I mean. We'll terrify it so much
it'll be beating its wings for mercy."

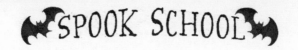

Lewis looked doubtful.

"Come on," I said, "we can do some gruesome, grisly things too, like make blood appear…"

"Oh no, not after last time," said Lewis.

"OK, we'll think of other terrifying stuff when we're there."

Lewis went on looking doubtful. "I'm going to have to think very carefully about this," he said, and went and sat on the roof of the railway station to be on his own. I was a bit cross about being left out, but I didn't say anything.

Finally, Lewis flew back and sat down next to me.

"I've come up with a better idea. We return tonight and say, 'We come in peace, and want to be friends with you'."

"We say this while it's chasing us around the house, do we?" I asked.

"We won't let it chase us because we won't run away from it. We'll smile at it and say, 'You can't scare us'."

I shook my head. "That won't work. My idea of really scaring it is much better."

"I disagree." Lewis stuck out his chin. "And as I am the leader, we'll do my plan. We'll tell it we come to make peace – not fight."

I shook my head. "It'll be a disaster."

"No it won't," said Lewis, "and stop arguing, I'm the leader."

"I still think you're wrong," I huffed. "But what does *my* opinion matter?"

Then it was time to go to sleep. All anyone passing would have seen was a wisp of morning mist hanging about the station platform. But really it was two spooks in dreamland.

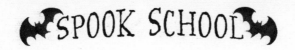

Later we became completely
invisible. Normally we'd have slept
until about five o'clock in the afternoon,
but for some reason I woke up early.
It had been a dull, drizzly November
day, and it was already dark.

Lewis slept on. I frowned. I knew
my plan was better than his, so why
didn't I put it into action now? I could
be there and back before Lewis had
even woken up.

A little voice told me I should wait
for Lewis … but a much louder one
told me to go now.

I hovered in the air for a few
moments, then I turned and flew
quickly back to the old, deserted house.
I stood outside and burped three times.

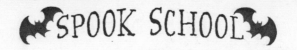

Mothman really was frightening. But I'd be ready for it this time.

I gave one more burp for luck – and then flew straight through the door.

Chapter Nine
The Talking Snow Globe

As I floated into the house I gave a loud "Whooo". Now there was a cry to make your hair stand on end. Mothman would certainly know that I was back.

On the little table by the front door was a snow globe – the kind that you shake to make it snow. It looked lonely there. And I felt like a bit of fun. So I concentrated and said, "Spook-rise." Instantly the snow globe rose up into the air. And to cheer things up I added, "Spook-dance." Soon it was swinging and darting about. I giggled. Oh, I do like a happy snow globe.

The snow globe and I swept into the kitchen. "Whooo," I cried. I liked doing that. So I said it again. "Whooo." Then I stopped. Standing right in

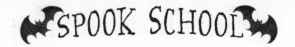

front of me was a white-haired woman.
Her eyes looked distinctly glassy.

Now, although she couldn't see me –
no human could unless I chose to show
myself – she'd have heard my eerie
cries all right. And she couldn't have
failed to notice the snow globe jiving
about in mid-air either.

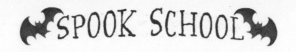

I realized the snow globe was worrying her a bit, so I said, "Spook-settle." The snow globe immediately floated to the edge of the kitchen table where it perched obediently, its snow swirling madly.

The woman was still doing her zombie impression. In fact, she was starting to worry me – I was afraid she might pass out – so I said, in my kindliest voice, "Don't be afraid."

But the woman took no notice. She opened her mouth to scream – but no sound came out. Then she stumbled back, her hands clutching her mouth. I really hoped she wasn't going to fall because I wouldn't have been able to catch her.

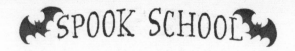

Suddenly I heard the rumble of voices. The back door opened and two men appeared. The younger one was saying, "Yes, the garden does need a little bit of work, and there's no electricity at present, but I hope you can see its potential. And the idea of this house being haunted is absolutely laughable…" Then he stopped.

The woman was now walking towards the door like a sleepwalker. "But it really is haunted," she shrieked.

The older man rushed over to her. "Florence my dear, what's happened?"

"Clive, you see that snow globe?"

He gazed at it and nodded.

"Well, it just flew in here as casually as you like, and then it started dancing."

The two men began to smile. "Don't you dare laugh, either of you," she screamed.

They immediately stopped.

"And then that snow globe spoke to me," she continued. "It said, 'Don't be afraid'."

"Perhaps it was just the wind howling," said Clive, putting his arm around her. "It's terrible out there."

The woman brushed his arm away. "I tell you, that snow globe spoke, just as clearly as you're talking now."

The men stared at poor Florence as if she'd gone mad. I decided to help. "Actually, it wasn't the snow globe who spoke it was me. And like I said before – don't be afraid, because…"

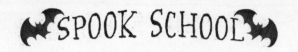

But I stopped here as Florence,
Clive and the estate agent weren't
listening to me any more. They were
all scrambling out of the front door as
fast as their legs could carry them. The
estate agent was shrieking even more
loudly than Florence.

I was a little disappointed by this
reaction, as I'd spoken to them in my
gentlest voice. Still, I suppose a chatty
snow globe could be a bit alarming.
As they ran yelling into the street they
didn't see another spook slip right
through them.

But I did.

It was Lewis.

Normally you couldn't find a
sunnier, happier spook than him.

But for once, he was looking absolutely furious. "What do you think you're doing?" he demanded.

"Ah well, I just thought I'd drop in," I explained.

"And try and frighten Mothman yourself."

"Yes," I admitted.

"But instead, you've just sent off three humans, scared out of their wits," said Lewis. "And you know we're not supposed to have any contact with humans without Spookmaster's permission."

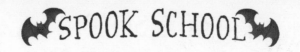

"I know, and I'm really sorry about scaring them. You see, I didn't think anyone was in here, except for Mothman, so I—"

"Sssh," interrupted Lewis. "Listen."

A second later I heard it too. A horrible, roaring sound, but quite different from what we'd heard last time.

This time it went, "Woooh, ha, ha," and, "Woooh, ha, ha," again.

"That's Mothman all right," said Lewis, looking at me. "Only this time I think it might be laughing."

Chapter Ten
Mothman's Secret

"Laughing?" I said, outraged.

"Yes, laughing," Lewis repeated. "At us!"

"I ought to punch it for that. It needs teaching a lesson." I flew off furiously.

"No, wait," said Lewis. "This time we'll face it together. And we'll do this my way."

We both flew upstairs and followed the noise of the laughing which, if anything, was getting even louder.

"It's in that bedroom," I said. "Probably hiding under the bed, and when we go in, it'll leap out at us."

"Well, we won't let Mothman scare us again, will we?" said Lewis.

"No," I cried loudly.

"Off we go then," said Lewis. "But let me do the talking."

We opened the bedroom door and immediately Mothman dived towards us. The feeling of terror rushed back.

Lewis hissed, "Don't move; remember it can't do anything to us."

I kept reminding myself of that and we stayed completely still as Mothman swooped nearer and nearer. Then it suddenly stopped – its awful smell

wafting over us – and it made that
very weird
sound again.

Wooon, Ha,ha,ha!

Lewis bowed politely and rather
bravely I thought, and said, "Good
evening, I hope you are not feeling
unwell." Then he whispered to me,
"It won't know what we're saying, but
my voice might reassure it."

To our amazement, Mothman
replied in a surprisingly young,

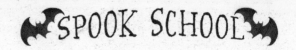

high-pitched voice. "Actually, I can understand every word you're saying."

We both gaped at it.

"You're a talking monster?" I asked.

"No, I'm not," said the voice. "Don't be silly." It sounded quite offended.

"What are you then?" asked Lewis.

"Watch." It was practically an order.

A thin mist wafted over us. Mothman disappeared. Then, before we knew what was going on – a new figure appeared. It was a girl, about the same age as us.

Lewis and I stared at each other. In a night of shocks this was the biggest shock of all. And the most embarrassing. We'd been scared out of our wits – by a girl!

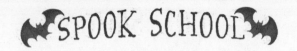

"But how?" began Lewis. "What are you doing here?"

"Oh, I've been a ghost for ages, ever since I passed over in fact," said the girl.

"But all children are taken to Spook School," said Lewis.

"I wasn't," said the girl. "They must have missed me. So I took over this house. I turned myself into a monster to scare strangers away."

"You did that all by yourself," said Lewis, "without any lessons?"

"Of course!" cried the girl. "It wasn't that hard. And I've had hours and hours to practise. But tonight when you," she pointed at me, "frightened away those people, it was just so funny,

I couldn't stop laughing. I haven't
had a good laugh like that for months."
Then she added politely, "Sorry if I
frightened you when you called
before."

"Oh, you didn't frighten me," I said
at once.

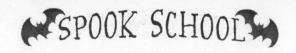

"We were just a bit surprised, that's all," said Lewis.

"You did some great sound effects … and that stinky smell," I said.

The girl smiled. "I know – I was very proud of that."

Lewis looked at her. "It must be lonely though, living here all by yourself."

She nodded and then said eagerly, "Do you want to haunt this house with me? I suppose I might let you."

"Oh no," interrupted Lewis and he explained about Spook School and why we were here. "Hey, why don't you come back with us?" he suggested.

She hesitated. "I don't know."

"You can always go back to your

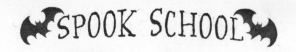

haunting later. But I think you'll love it at Spook School – and you're clearly very talented," said Lewis. "I mean, I can't change shape – and neither can Charlie, can you?"

"No," I agreed but added, "Not that I've tried it yet."

"So say yes," Lewis urged her.

"Before you do that tell us your name," I asked, "because we can't go on calling you Mothman."

"Is that what you called me?" She started to laugh again. I think she'd been very lonely indeed. "My name is Ella – and yes, I will come back with you; for a little while anyway."

We soon arrived back at Spook School, landing at the place I'd first arrived, at the top of the hill.

"This is going to be so great," said Lewis excitedly.

"We'll be heroes," I cried.

Ella stared at her new surroundings. "I want to go home," she said. We both turned a somersault with shock.

"But why?" asked Lewis. "You'll be

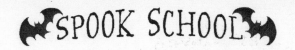

famous. Everyone will want to meet
the girl who got missed off the list of
spooks—"

"And turned herself into Mothman
instead," I interrupted. "And you've got
to meet Spookmaster."

"I haven't *got* to do anything," cried
Ella.

Lewis and I frowned at each other.
Then Lewis said, "But you can't go
until you've met Star."

"Who's Star?" she demanded.

"He's my invisible horse," said
Lewis. He gave a whistle.

There was a faint clatter of hooves.

"But there's nothing there,"
exclaimed Ella.

"Oh yes there is," said Lewis.

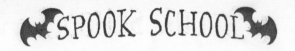

"Stretch out your hand."

Very puzzled, she reached out and then her face lit up. "Oh yes, I can feel him now. There's a good boy. But why is he invisible?"

"Because he hasn't got the power to make anyone see him," explained Lewis.

The howl for the start of school began, making Ella leap up into the air.

"Don't worry," I said, "that howl gave me a shock the first time I heard it. It just means lessons are beginning."

"And you can ride Star to school," said Lewis.

"Can I really?" Ella cried excitedly.

Lewis nodded.

Without another word Ella jumped on to the horse. She seemed to have

forgotten all about leaving now, and
she rode away with the biggest smile
on her face. "So there goes Mothman
riding away on Star," I said.

Lewis grinned at me. "I wonder
what our next incredible adventure's
going to be, Charlie?"

"I don't know,"
I replied. "But
I can't wait to
find out."

Jokes

(FOR GHOULISH FOLK)

What should a short-sighted ghost have? Spooktacles!

What does a hungry ghost want?

Ice scream!

Ha ha!

Where do ghosts pick up their mail? At the ghost office!

Catch up with Charlie in his next spooky adventure:

And find out more
about Pete Johnson at:

www.petejohnsonauthor.com